Fluttershy's
Secret Song

ORCHARD

Fluttershy loves animals. Her cutie mark is three pink butterflies.

Big Mac is quiet but very strong. His cutie mark is a green apple.

Rarity is a glamorous Unicorn. Her cutie mark is three blue diamonds.

Twilight Sparkle is learning all about magic. Her cutie mark is a pink star.

Pinkie Pie gives the best parties EVER and loves to make everyone laugh. Her cutie mark is three bouncing balloons.

Applejack works on a farm. Her cutie mark is three red apples.

Rainbow Dash is a fast Pegasus pony. She helps to control the weather. Her cutie mark is a cloud with a rainbow lightning bolt.

Spike the dragon is Twilight Sparkle's assistant.

Contents

✶ ✶ ✶

Part One
A Shy Singer

Chapter One
A Morning Song

It was a lovely morning in
Ponyville. Fluttershy opened
the window of her cottage and
sang to all her animal friends.
Fluttershy had a beautiful
voice, and her song made all
the animals feel very happy.

It even made a sleepy old bear
smile!

Fluttershy did not realise
that her best friends Twilight
Sparkle, Rainbow Dash,
Rarity, Pinkie Pie and
Applejack had come to visit.

They heard her singing. They
did not know that Fluttershy
could sing so well!

"That was like a little slice of
heaven!" said Applejack.

"You must join our
singing group!" cried Rarity.

"You can sing with us when we perform at the concert tomorrow night. The show is at the pet centre."

Rarity sang with three other ponies in a singing group called the Ponytones. They were all great singers!

"I can't join the Ponytones!" said Fluttershy. "Singing in front of a crowd is my worst nightmare."

Fluttershy had stage fright. That meant she was scared to perform in front of other ponies.

"But I will come and watch you sing," Fluttershy told Rarity.

Rarity shook her head sadly. She wished she could convince Fluttershy to sing on stage.

Chapter Two

Poorly Pony

There was a lot to do before
the concert. Fluttershy was
organising the event. She hoped
that everyone who came to
the concert would adopt a new
pet so that all of the animals in
Ponyville had a loving home.

Fluttershy was very busy blowing up balloons, arranging cakes and hanging up pretty bunting. As she worked, the Ponytones arrived to practise their song. Applejack's brother, Big Mac, was in the group too.

Fluttershy didn't feel brave enough to be on stage with the singing group, but she loved listening to them.

Fluttershy listened to Rarity and the three other Ponytones rehearsing their song.

Fluttershy started to wish she
could join the group … but she
was just too scared to perform
in front of a crowd.

Fluttershy went to check
on the animals, but when she
came back, all the Ponytones

were looking miserable. Big
Mac had lost his voice! He had
a sore throat and he couldn't
sing at all. The Ponytones
needed all four singers in the
group so they could make the
songs sound perfect.

"But if the Ponytones don't perform, the Pet Centre Concert will be a disaster!" gasped Fluttershy. What were they going to do …?

Chapter Three
Magic Medicine

Suddenly Fluttershy had a
brilliant idea! They would
visit Zecora. Zecora was a
mysterious zebra who lived
deep in the Everfree Forest. She
might have a special medicine
to make Big Mac's voice better.

"This pony will be fine, but it will take a bit of time!" Zecora told Rarity and Fluttershy. Oh no! There was no way that the poor pony would be better in time for the performance at the Pet Centre Concert.

Fluttershy knew she had to do something to save the day. She decided that she would sing with the Ponytones. She already knew all of their songs. "I will do anything for the animals!" she cried.

"Wow! You'll even appear on stage with us!" cried Rarity in delight.

"Oh no, I can't do that," Fluttershy replied quickly. She had such bad stage fright she didn't feel that she could perform in front of an audience.

But how could she sing without being seen?

Then Rarity had an amazing idea. Fluttershy would stand behind a curtain and sing. The four Ponytones would be on the stage in front of the curtain.

Nobody would be able to see
Fluttershy so they wouldn't
know she was singing!

Fluttershy thought this was
a brilliant plan … but would it
really work?

Part Two
Fluttershy has FUN!

Chapter Four

Time for the Ponytones!

That evening, all the ponies in Ponyville were at the Pet Centre Concert. Lots of pets found new homes. Everyone was having a wonderful time. Soon, it was time for the Ponytones to perform.

Fluttershy was hidden behind the curtain at the back of the stage. She took a deep breath. When the music started, she started to sing along with the Ponytones.

Fluttershy sounded amazing!

She even started to enjoy herself. She didn't feel shy or scared because the audience couldn't see her.

The crowd clapped and cheered. The concert was a huge success.

"We loved the show so much! Will you come and sing at our daughter's birthday party tomorrow?" asked two friendly ponies. "It will really make her day special!"

"Um," Rarity said.

Fluttershy had only joined the Ponytones so the Pet Centre Concert show would be a success. Rarity was about to say no. But then Fluttershy whispered to Rarity, "I'll sing if I can stay behind the curtain."

Rarity nodded.

Fluttershy was excited about singing with the Ponytones again. She was having fun!

Chapter Five

Secret Singer

The next day the Ponytones sang at the young filly's birthday party. Fluttershy hid behind the curtain again, secretly singing. She did an amazing job. This time she felt even more confident.

She danced around happily as she sang.

"We love the Ponytones! We love the Ponytones!" cried the crowd of excited young ponies. Everyone was dancing and enjoying the music!

The Mayor of Ponyville
was watching the birthday
performance. After the show
had finished she came to speak
to the Ponytones. "That was
amazing! I enjoyed the show
so much," she said to them.

"I'd love you to perform at
a ceremony tomorrow. It
would make it such a special
occasion!"

Once again, Rarity was
about to tell the mayor that the
Ponytones couldn't perform.

She didn't want Fluttershy to
have to be a secret singer over
and over again!

But Fluttershy wanted to
sing. "We wouldn't want to
disappoint the mayor!" she
whispered.

So Rarity agreed that the Ponytones would perform for the mayor.

Rarity thought Fluttershy was really enjoying singing in the group. If only she didn't have to hide.

Chapter Six
Another Day, Another Concert

The next day the Ponytones
performed at the mayor's
ceremony. A big crowd turned
out to watch them! This
time there was no curtain
for Fluttershy to hide behind.
Instead, she hid in a barrel and

happily sang the songs.

Each time Fluttershy sang with the Ponytones, she enjoyed it more and more. She found herself dancing around and adding more notes and tones to the songs each time!

The audience loved the shows and each and every day new ponies asked the Ponytones to perform for them. Next the group sang for the spa ponies and then they sang for a whole class of school ponies!

That night, as the Ponytones prepared to sing at a party, Rarity and Big Mac came to talk to Fluttershy.

"Fluttershy, we have some great news! We don't need you to sing any more," Rarity said.

"Big Mac is feeling much better. His voice has come back!"

The Ponytones thought that Fluttershy would be pleased not to have to sing any more. But Fluttershy felt very sad.

"It's just I didn't know that the last show was my last performance ever!" she sighed. "I'd love to sing just one more time …"

Part Three
A Secret Revealed ...

Chapter Seven

Fluttershy Faces Her Fears

Rarity and the Ponytones hated to see kind Fluttershy looking so sad.

"Of course you must sing with the Ponytones one last time," said Rarity. "Thank you for all your help!"

Fluttershy was delighted. She was determined to enjoy her last secret performance.

Behind the curtain that night, Fluttershy sang her heart out and added more and more new notes and words to the song.

Fluttershy was having such an amazing time dancing that she didn't notice when she kicked the curtain down. The curtain fell on top of the Ponytones. Everyone gasped as they saw Fluttershy singing!

She was amazing!

As soon as Fluttershy saw
that everyone was looking
at her, she felt very scared!
After all, performing in front
of everyone was her worst
nightmare.

Even though the crowd was cheering and clapping and calling her name, Fluttershy panicked and galloped away. She just wanted to be left alone!

Chapter Eight
Truth Time

"Poor Fluttershy was too scared to let everyone see her sing!" cried Applejack. "We need to tell her what a great singer she is!"

Fluttershy's friends rushed off to find her.

"That was unbelievable!" cried Pinkie Pie, when they finally found Fluttershy.

But Fluttershy wouldn't listen. "I'm glad you enjoyed it," she said. "But I'm never going to sing in front of anyone again.

It's so scary!"

Kind Twilight Sparkle smiled at Fluttershy. "But what was so bad about it?" she asked gently. "Everyone cheering for you and saying what a wonderful singer you are?"

As Fluttershy looked around
her at her best friends in the
world, she thought about
what they were saying. The
truth was, singing in front
of everyone had not been
that bad!

Chapter Nine

A New Ponytone!

A few days later Fluttershy performed on stage with the Ponytones for the very first time! As she sang, she realised how amazing it was to be singing with the group rather than hiding!

Her best friends watched her sing and smiled when they saw how happy she looked.

"You did it, Fluttershy!" cheered Rainbow Dash.

"And you didn't look scared, even though we were all staring at you!" giggled Pinkie Pie, giving Fluttershy a hug.

"Now you're not scared any more, will you sing with the Ponytones when we play at the Apple Family's party next week?" asked Rarity.

"OK," smiled Fluttershy.

Fluttershy realised that she had learnt a very important lesson. Being afraid had stopped her from doing what she really loved – singing! But, with a little help from her best friends, she had faced her fear.

And now Fluttershy's singing
could be enjoyed by everyone!

The End

There's lots of colouring, sticker and activity fun with My Little Pony!